A *Smudge* Book

Stop Bugging Me

But that's
what friends
are for.

DANIEL CLEARY

BLUE APPLE

Smudge, Where, are you going?

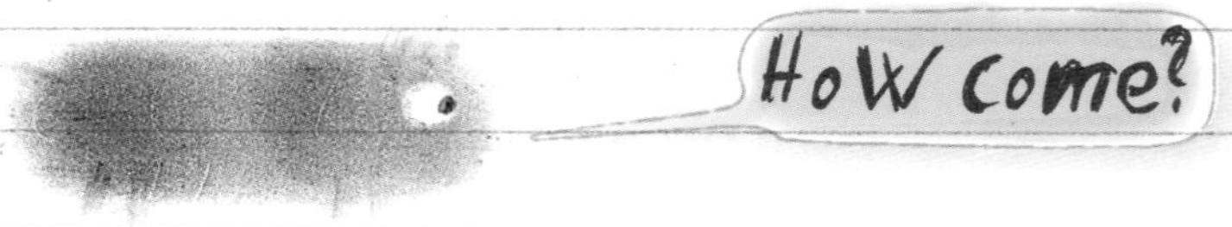
HoW come?

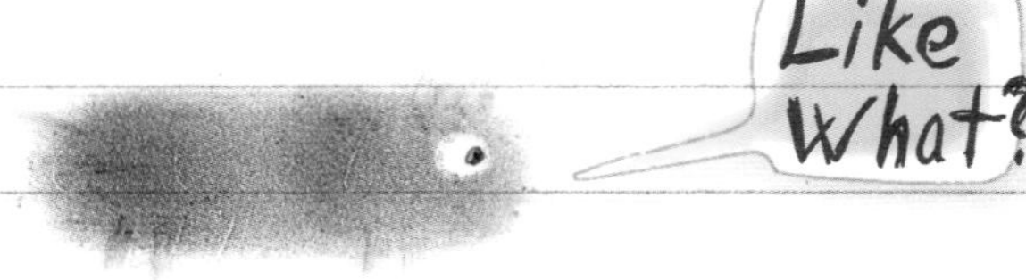
Like What?

Hi, Piggie. Hello, Smudge. Off somewhere interesting? May I tag along?
Oh, hi Fuzzie. Umm...

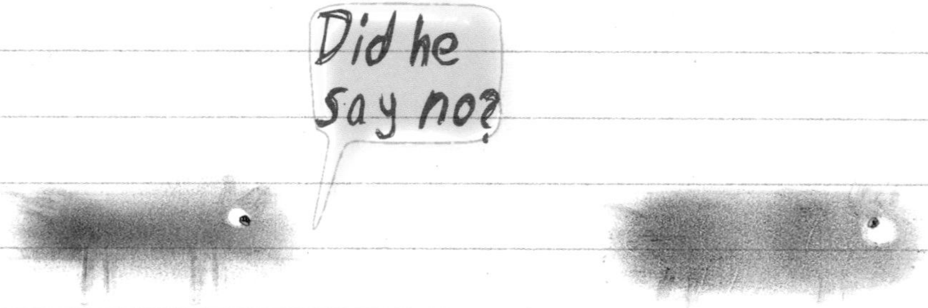
Did he say no?

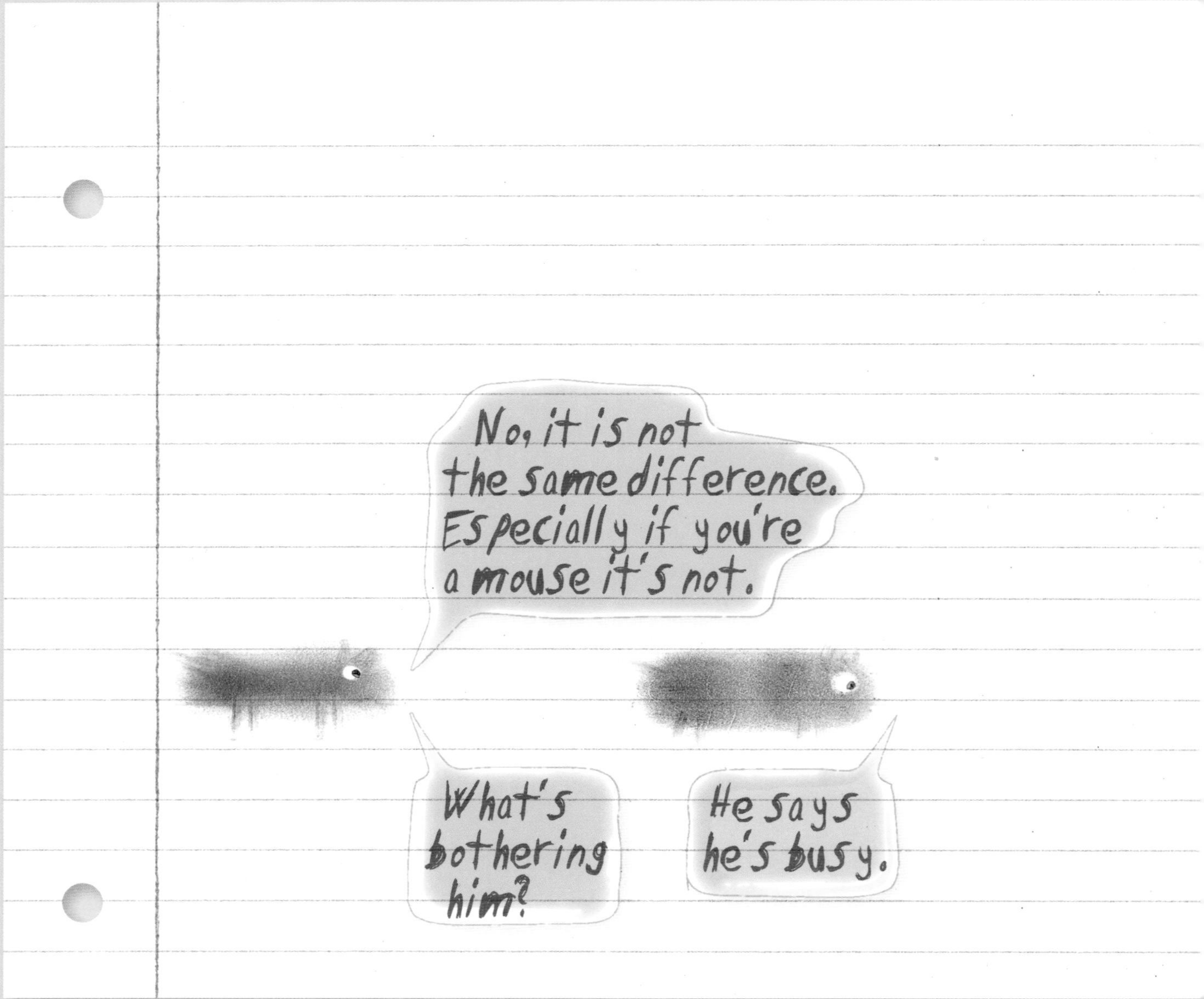
No, it is not the same difference. Especially if you're a mouse it's not.
What's bothering him?
He says he's busy.

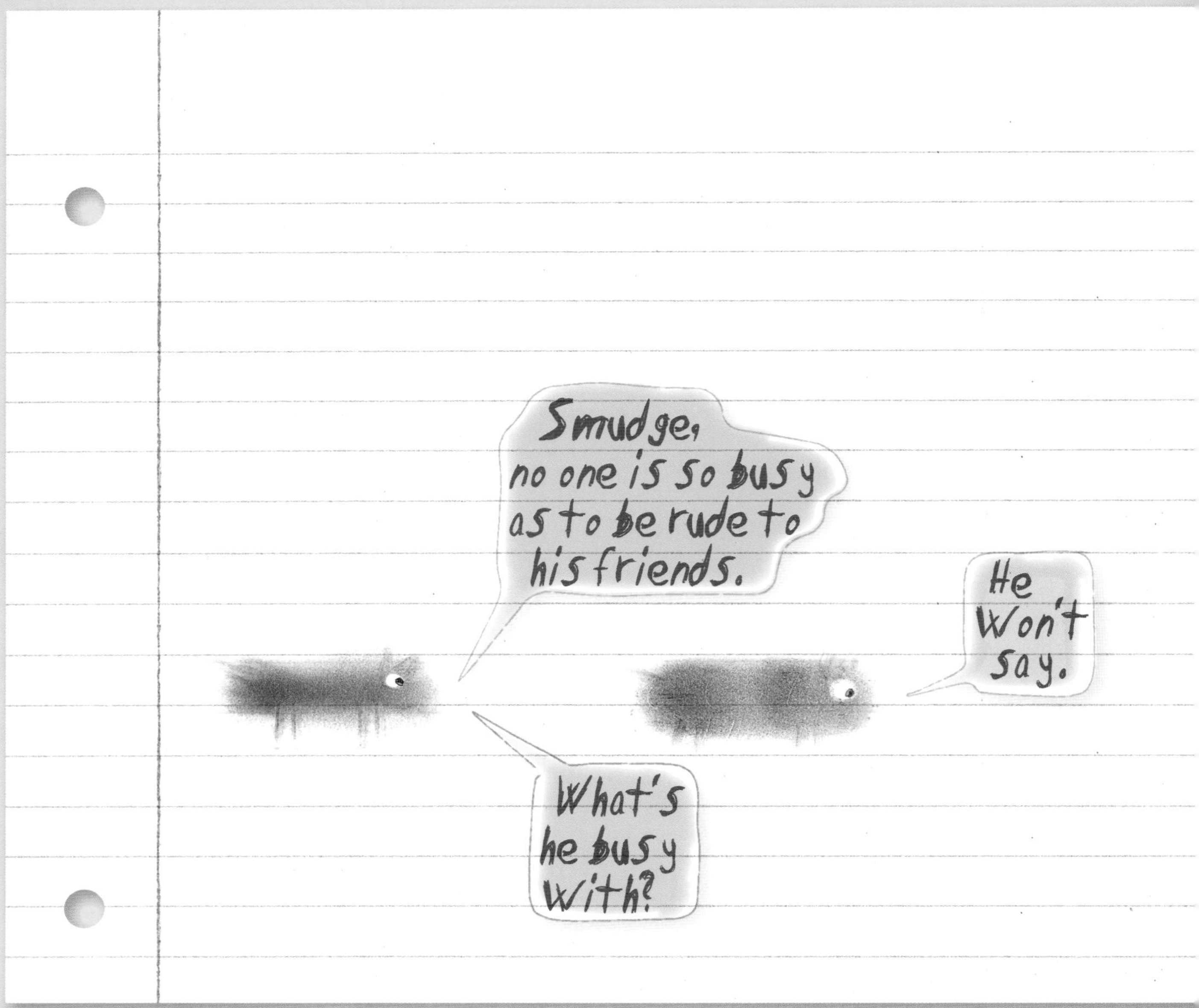
Smudge, no one is so busy as to be rude to his friends.
What's he busy with?
He won't say.

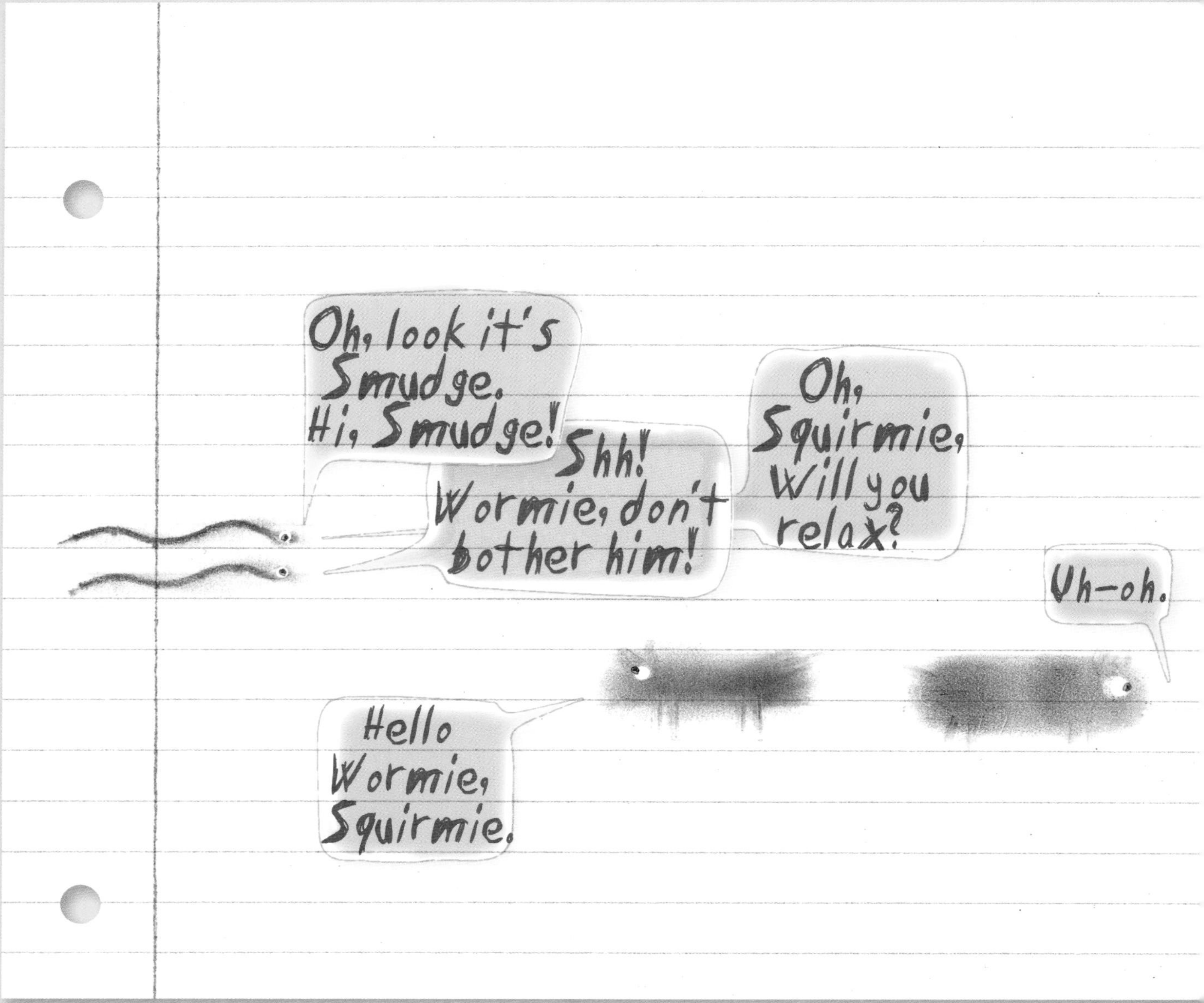
Oh, look it's Smudge. Hi, Smudge!
Shh! Wormie, don't bother him!
Oh, Squirmie, Will you relax?
Uh-oh.
Hello Wormie, Squirmie.

Terrific.
Worms.

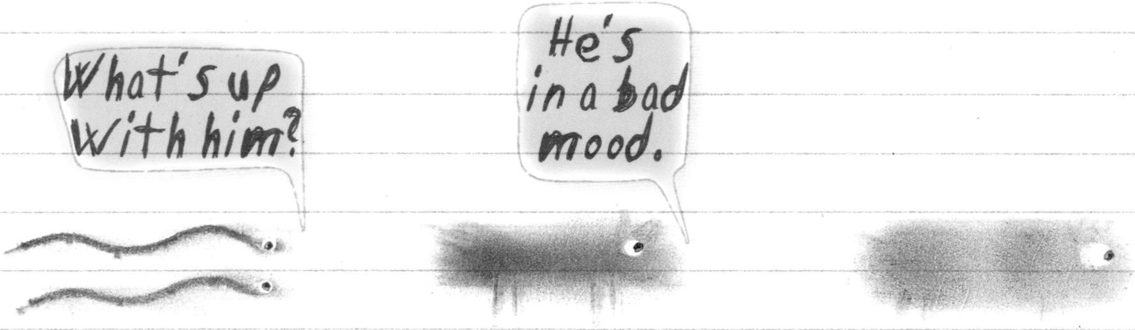
What's up with him?
He's in a bad mood.

I'm not in a bad mood! Sometimes a person needs a little privacy is all and doesn't like being chased by a guinea pig, a fuzzy mouse, and a noisy pair of twin worms!

Did he call us noisy?
Wormie, don't make a fuss!
It sounds to me like someone woke up on the wrong side of his dog bed!

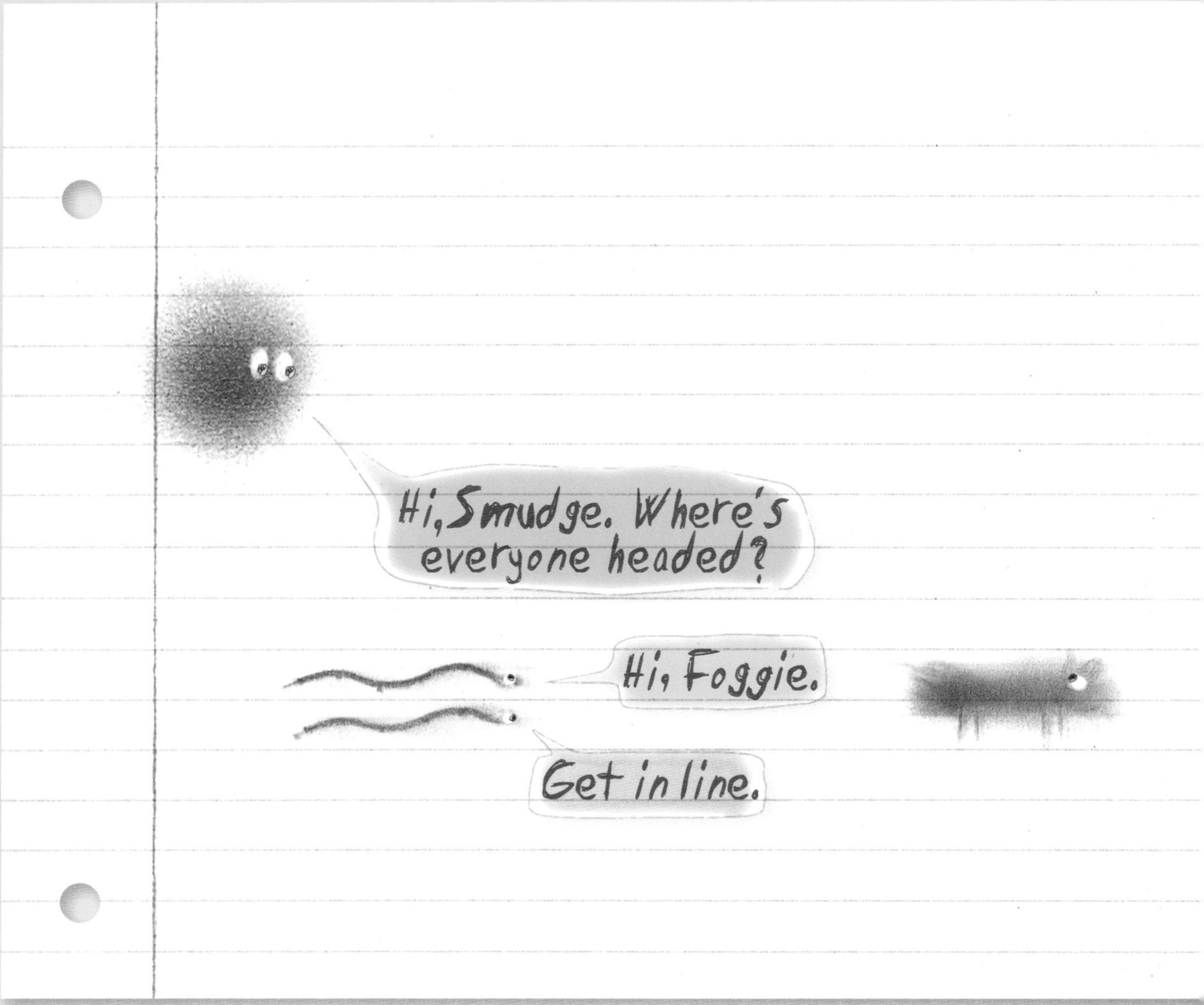
Hi, Smudge. Where's everyone headed?
Hi, Foggie.
Get in line.

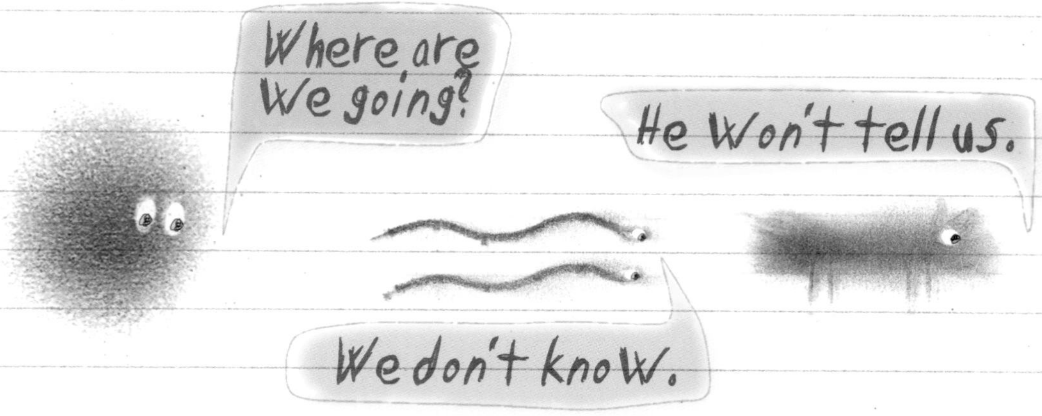
Where are we going?
He won't tell us.
We don't know.

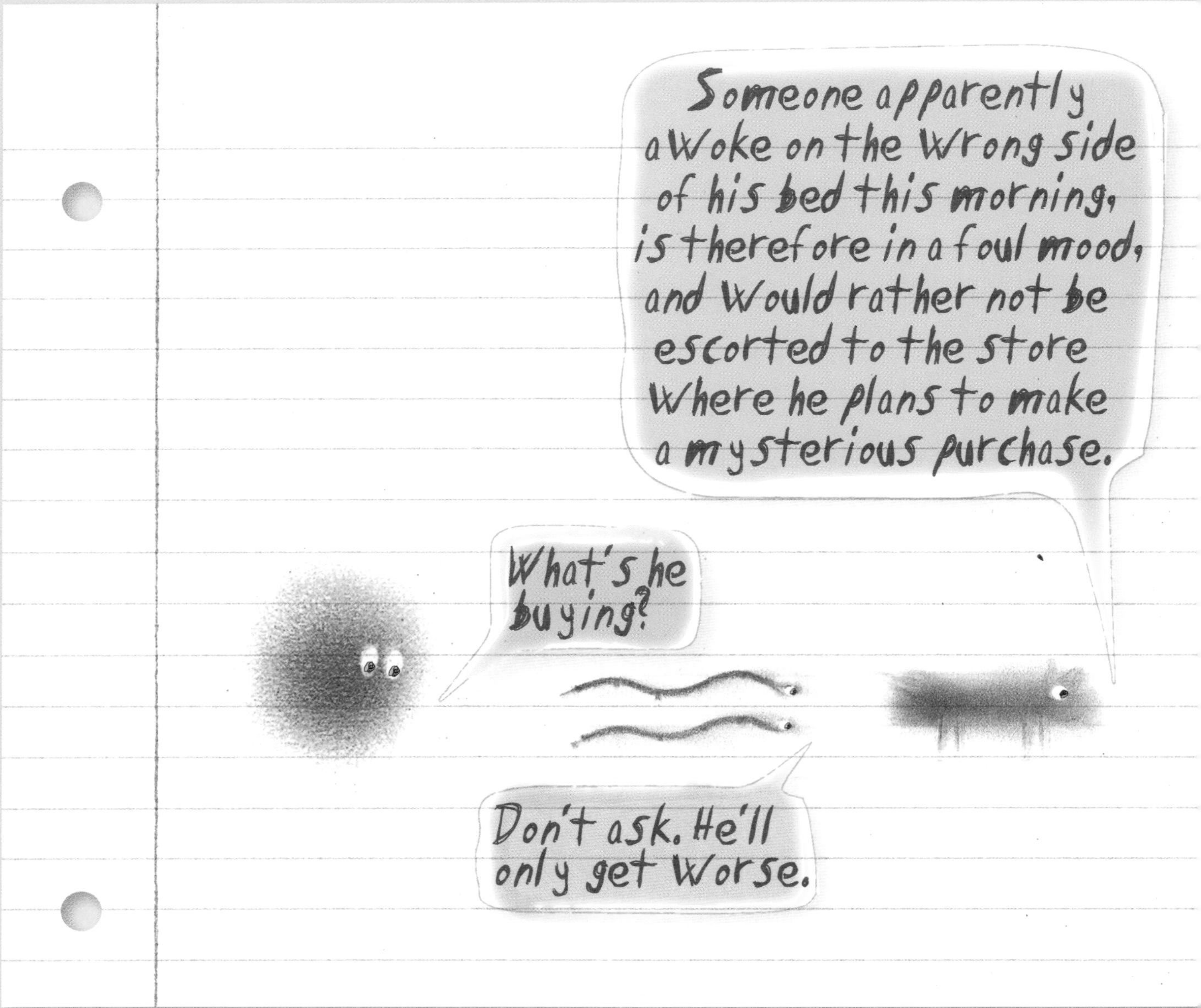
Someone apparently awoke on the wrong side of his bed this morning, is therefore in a foul mood, and would rather not be escorted to the store where he plans to make a mysterious purchase.
What's he buying?
Don't ask. He'll only get worse.

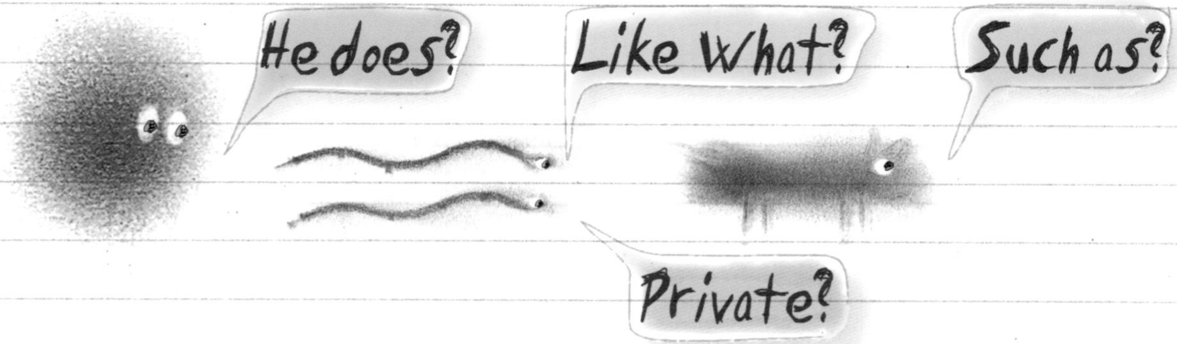
He does?
Like What?
Such as?
Private?

Underpants? Did he say, underpants?
That's all?
This is about underpants?
That's what he said.

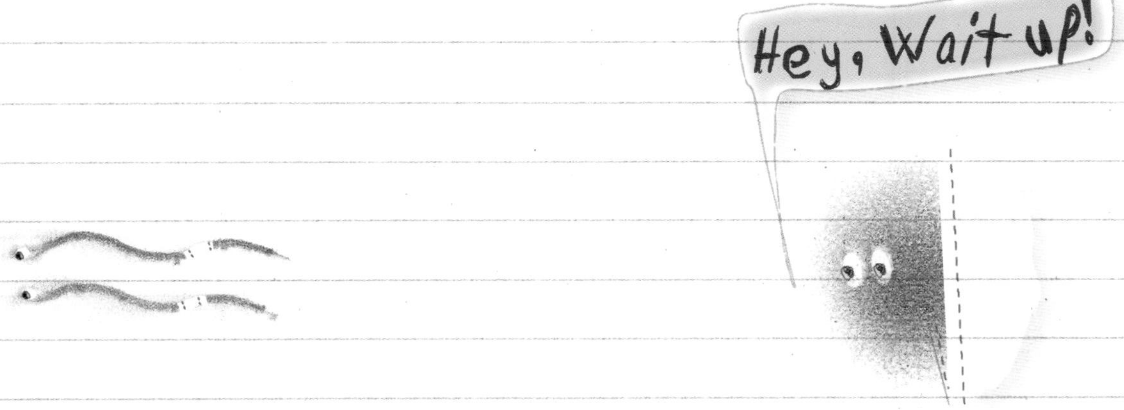
Hey, Wait up!

1 3 5 7 9 10 8 6 4 2